Twas the Night before Christmas: A Visit from St. Nicholas

Clement Clarke Moore

Clement Clarke Moore

Clement Clarke Moore (July 15, 1779 – July 10, 1863) was an American Professor of Oriental and Greek Literature, as well as Divinity and Biblical Learning, at the General Theological Seminary of the Protestant Episcopal Church, in New York City. Located on land donated by the "Bard of Chelsea" himself, the seminary still stands today on Ninth Avenue between 20th and 21st Streets, in an area known as Chelsea Square. Moore's connection with that institution continued for over twenty-five years. He is thought to be the author of the Christmas poem "A Visit from St. Nicholas", which later became famous as "'Twas the Night Before Christmas", but debate continues as to who really wrote it.

Twas the Night before Christmas

Twas the night before Christmas, when all through the house
Not a creature was stirring, not even a mouse;
The stockings were hung by the chimney with care
In hopes that St. Nicholas soon would be there;

The children were nestled all snug in their beds,

While visions of sugar-plums danced in their heads;
And mamma in her kerchief, and I in my cap,
Had just settled our brains for a long winter's nap,

When out on the lawn there arose such a clatter,
I sprang from the bed to see what was the matter.
Away to the window I flew like a flash,
Tore open the shutters and threw up the sash.

The moon on the breast of the new-fallen snow
Gave the lustre of mid-day to objects below,
When, what to my wondering eyes should appear,
But a miniature sleigh, and eight tiny reindeer,

With a little old driver, so lively and quick,

I knew in a moment it must be St. Nick.

More rapid than eagles his coursers they came,

And he whistled, and shouted, and called them by name:

Now, Dasher! now, Dancer! now, Prancer and Vixen!

On, Comet! on, Cupid! on, Donder and Blitzen!

To the top of the porch! to the top of the wall!

Now dash away! dash away! dash away all!"

As dry leaves that before the wild hurricane fly,
When they meet with an obstacle, mount to the sky;
So up to the house-top the coursers they flew,

With the sleigh full of Toys, and St. Nicholas too.

And then, in a twinkling, I heard on the roof
The prancing and pawing of each little hoof.
As I drew in my head, and was turning around,
Down the chimney St. Nicholas came with a bound.

He was dressed all in fur, from his

head to his foot,
And his clothes were all tarnished with ashes and soot;

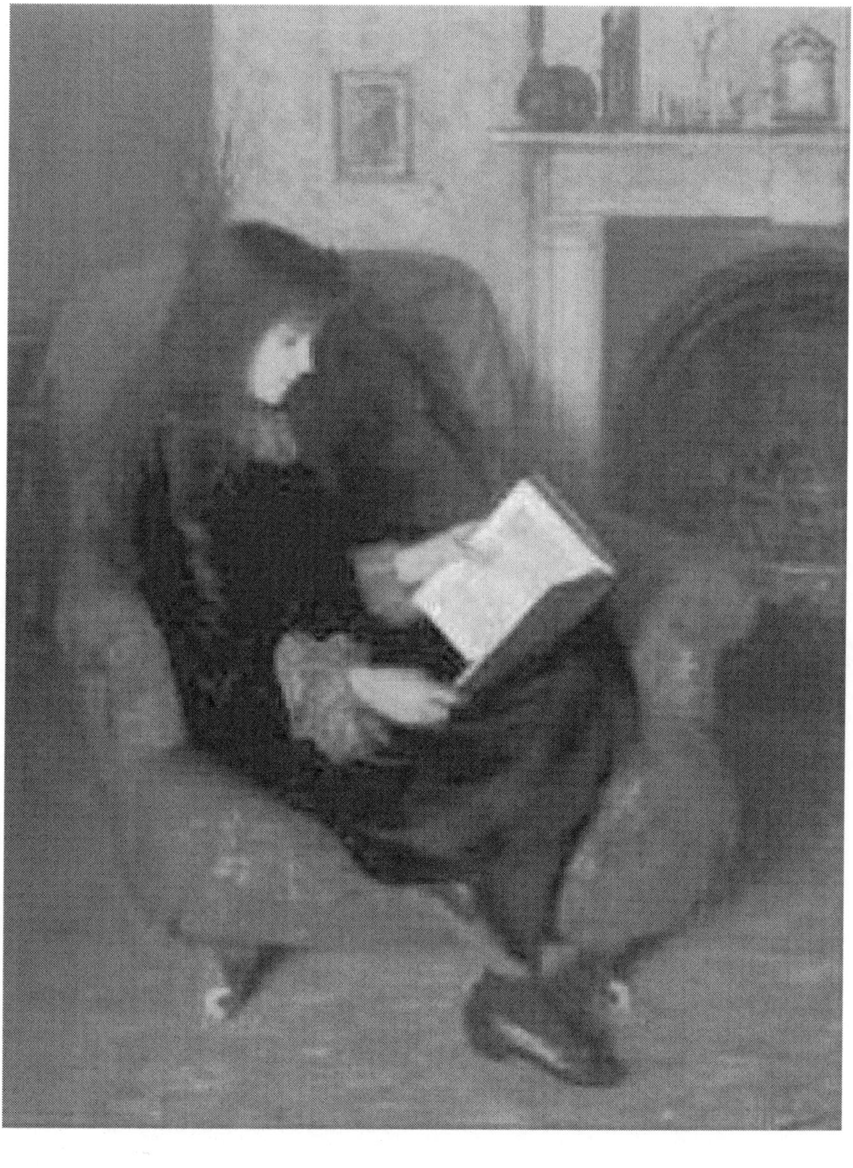

A bundle of Toys he had flung on his back,
And he looked like a peddler just opening his pack.

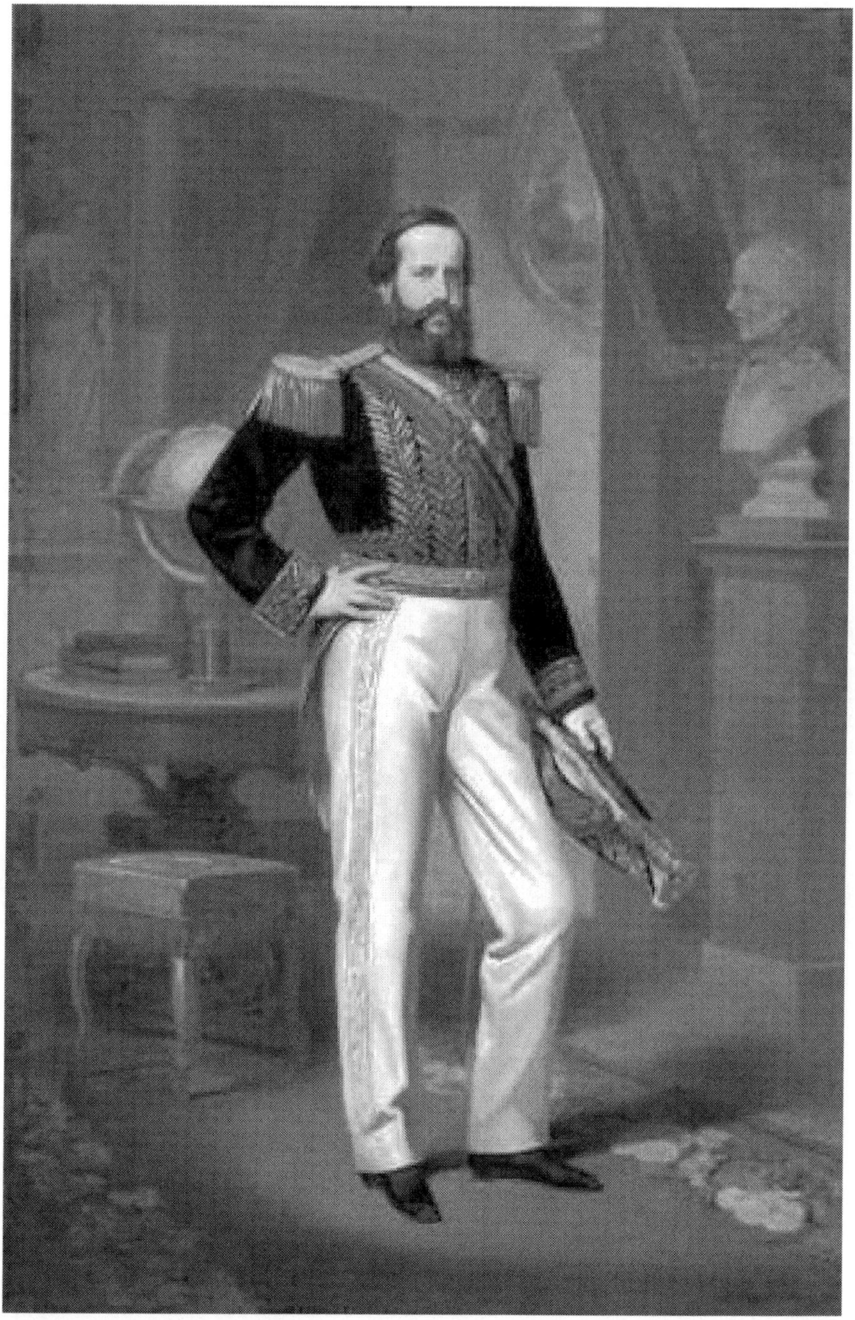

His eyes—how they twinkled! his dimples how merry!
His cheeks were like roses, his nose like a cherry!
His droll little mouth was drawn up like a bow,
And the beard of his chin was as white as the snow;

The stump of a pipe he held tight in his teeth,
And the smoke it encircled his head like a wreath;
He had a broad face and a little round belly,
That shook when he laughed, like a bowlful of jelly.

He was chubby and plump, a right jolly old elf,
And I laughed when I saw him, in spite of myself;
A wink of his eye and a twist of

his head,
Soon gave me to know I had nothing to dread;

He spoke not a word, but went straight to his work,
And filled all the stockings; then turned with a jerk,

And laying his finger aside of his nose,
And giving a nod, up the chimney he rose;

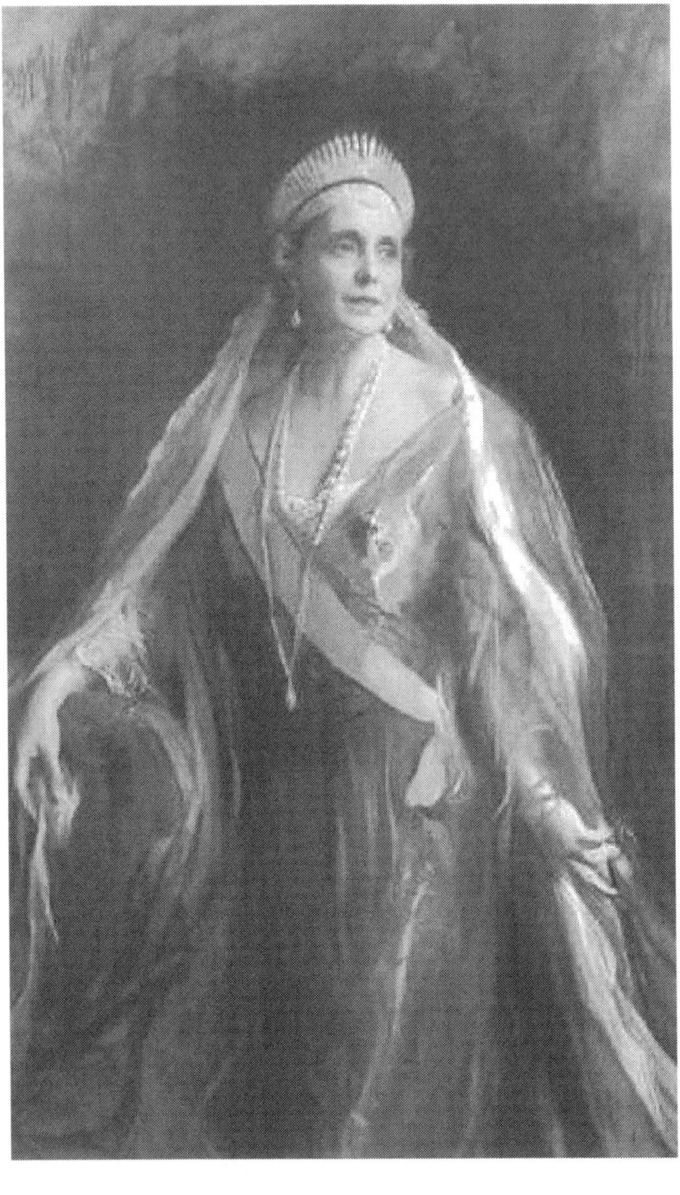

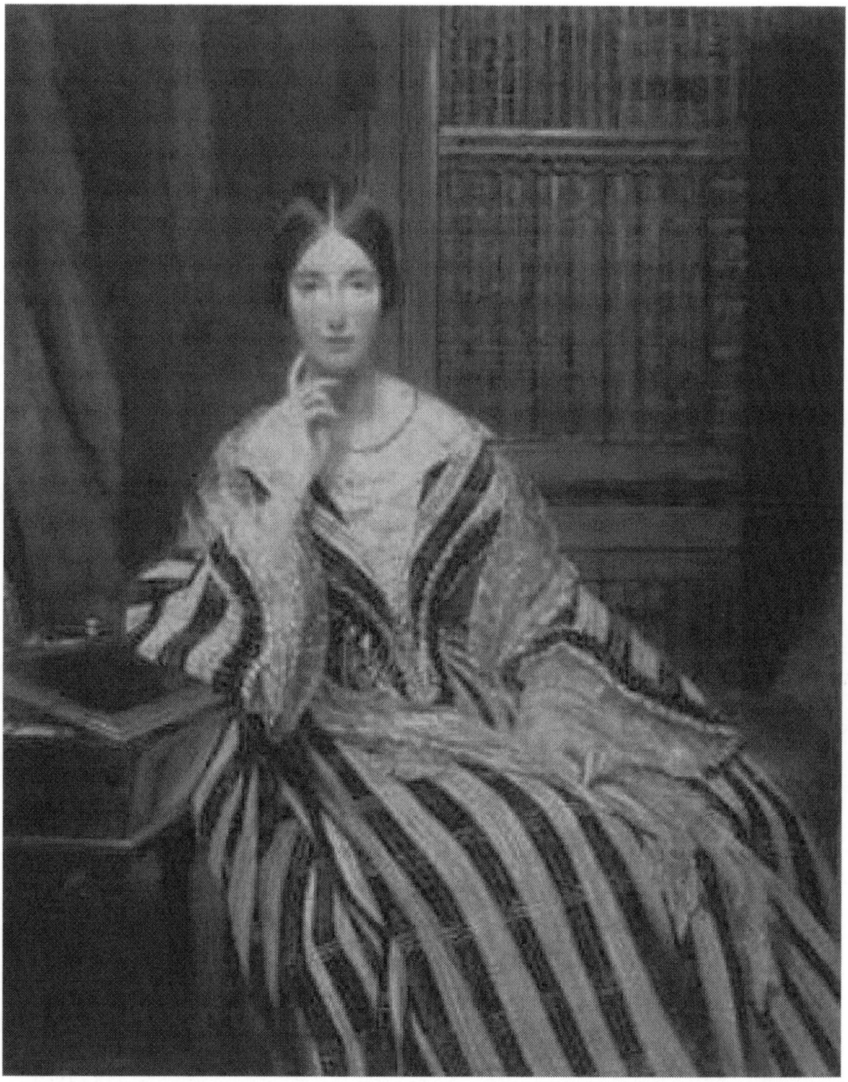

He sprang to his sleigh, to his team gave a whistle,
And away they all flew like the down of a thistle.
But I heard him exclaim, ere he drove out of sight,
"Happy Christmas to all, and to all a good-night."

All rights reserved.

All Rights Reserved. No part of this publication may be reproduced in any form or by any means, including scanning, photocopying, or otherwise without prior written permission of the copyright holder.

Disclaimer and Terms of Use: The Author and Publisher have strived to be as accurate and complete as possible in the creation of this book, notwithstanding the fact that he does not warrant or represent at any time that the contents within are accurate due to the rapidly changing nature of the Internet. While all attempts have been made to verify information provided in this publication, the Author and Publisher assume no responsibility for errors, omissions, or contrary interpretation of the subject matter herein. Any perceived slights of specific persons, people, or organizations are unintentional. In practical advice books, like anything else in life, there are no guarantees of results. Readers are cautioned to rely on their own judgment about their individual circumstances and act accordingly. This book is not intended for use as a source of legal, medical, business, accounting or financial advice. All readers are advised to seek the services of competent professionals in the legal, medical, business, accounting, and finance fields.

Printed in Poland
by Amazon Fulfillment
Poland Sp. z o.o., Wrocław

MEN OF DUST, MEN OF GLORY

In this book, JT encourages Christian men that even though we are "men of dust" - flesh and blood, frail and weak, prone to sin and destined to die - we don't need to be doomed to live such a diminished life. Jesus descended to where we live, so that we can ascend to where He lives. Jesus dwelled in our dust, so that we can dwell in His glory. With Jesus' help, men can turn from being dust-dwellers to being glory-dwellers.

That's some destiny!

BEHOLD THE MAN

What does it mean to be a real man in today's world? In this passionately argued book, we go back to the first century AD and present two very different ideas of manhood and masculinity – one provided by Caesar and the other provided by Christ. Christ advocated the power of love. Caesar exhibited the love of power.

Written with raw honesty, this book encourages men to adopt an intelligent and heartfelt radicalism that has a culture-changing capacity.

FREEDOM FIGHTERS

Being a real man means being a freedom fighter - fighting for our own freedom and for the freedom of those we influence. You will learn what it takes to be a Christian man in a world where the values of heaven are more needed than ever before.

The whole world is waiting for such men. Wives are waiting. Sons and daughters are waiting. Orphans and widows are waiting. Troubled teens are waiting. Slaves and refugees are waiting. Let the real men arise!

123

GET IN THE GALLEY AND ROW